Sensual Love

SCRIPTOR HOUSE
The Epitome of Greatness

T.S.E BEAUMONT

Scriptor House LLC
2810 N Church St Wilmington, Delaware, 19802
www.scriptorhouse.com
Phone: +1302-205-2043

Paperback ISBN: 979-8-88692-170-0
eBook ISBN: 979-8-88692-171-7

The Art of Sensual Love

(Tantric poetry for the soul)

By T.S.E Beaumont

Shield of Love.

This love is my shield from the cruelty of this world.

This love is my greatest defender & my greatest hope.

This love fills me with absolution, with peace,
with hope & with abundance.

This love wraps me in his loving arms & cradles me,
protecting me as would protect a small child
from danger of from the dark.

This love strikes a match and lights the candle,
which has become the torch and shining beacon of
dreams, hopes, aspirations and desires.

In truth, we are all wounded children
that need protection, care and love.

We all want to return to womb of loving protection
and warmth.

We want to be blissful safe, secure, lovingly nurtured
and cared for.

We want the steady heartbeat of love, the gentle
swooshing of the water of life.

We want to feel the softness and velvety enveloping
silken splendours of lives passage into this world.

We want to be touched deeply, with sensuality, with
understanding, with great passionate lust.

With an unbearable yearning to consume & be
consumed wholly, entirely, completely by the rhapsodic
symphonic energy and creation force of this life.

To bath in the pure nectar of the sweetest existence in
the divine feminine channel of life.

For the masculine to grow, to live with vigour,
strength, power and alchemical force of conception.

As we recover & grow from the reasons, the lessons,
the mistakes, the seasons of our lives.

It's true we must hold no regrets, yet it is also true that
we should remain inactive and inert.

We need to channel a creative response.

To leave beauty from the pain & disgust.

To alchemise.

We need to rise & respond to lives challenges as they
are encountered.

We need to face life head on.

The most important lesson is to love yourself.

All the foibles, all the flaws, all the vulnerability of
being a fragile human flower of this earth.

And yet never lose sight of the gorgeousness &
ethereal divinity of your soaring Godlike soul.

We are bound to heaven & earth, to yin & yang.

To badness & goodness.

To hate & love.

To failure & to triumphs.

To sinners & saints.

I never faltered when I know that this love is
real & true.

This is a bubble of love and whirl of bliss.

The beauty of this will be sealed with a kiss.

T.S.E Beaumont

Seeing.

Love is not blind.

Love sees.

Love sees all.

Love sees everything.

Love sees me.

Love sees you.

Love sees him.

Love sees the pain.

Love sees the truth.

Love sees the anxiety.

Love see the hurt.

Love sees the fear.

Love sees the challenges.

Love sees the best.

Love sees the past.

Love sees the future.

Love sees the now.

Love sees the sky.

Love sees the air.

Love sees the wind.

Love sees the rain.

Love sees the sun.

Love sees the moon.

Love sees the birds.

Love sees the trees.

Love sees the garden.

Love sees the bees.

Love sees the beauty.

Love sees the grace.

Love sees the wonderful smile upon your face.

Love sees the vision.

Loves sees the paradigm.

Love sees opportunities.

Love sees the artistry.

Love sees the music.

Love sees the triumph.

Love sees infinite galaxies of just me & you.

I see your face and my heart expands in explosive
response of love.

This love I feel for you has not diminished.

It has enhanced & grown over the years.

It feels more vast than the universe, has greater depth than the deepest oceans, it is more magnificent than the brightest nebula, it shines brighter than the sun, more mysterious than an eclipse.

You fill me with endless bountiful love, nurturing & goodness.

Your love sees me. My love sees you.

This love sees the future and infinite possibilities for us two.

T.S.E Beaumont

Sensuality.

When you truly love someone adore them.

Appreciate who you fell in love with, then
never forget.

Love growths in appreciation.

It's a soul evolution & a journey to more experienced
life. Be comfortable with the one you love, appreciate
their naturalness & their quirky habits.

Love them like you would your own children.
Unconditionally & infinitely.

Appreciate them completely, the beautiful rugged
handsomeness or the more refined version.

Love every articulation of who they want to become.

Listen to them, want to really understand them.

When they are quiet have a desire to know why &
support in silence or by talking it out.

Be a blanket of lovingly comfort & glorious intimacy.

Nestle in the tenderness of their affection.

Laugh at their comedic goofing off.

Savour those messy mornings of whimsical happiness
& endless kissing.

See the exquisite beauty in the flaws of character.

Relish seeing them in mismatched pjs & beanie in the
cold of winter.

Luxuriate in the salty, silken, sultry heat of
summertime sleeping & sensual seduction.

Let them touch you everywhere, your body is as
sacred, as this love.

Lie on the grass together & stare at the cloudscapes.

Swim in the ocean, skin to skin & kiss with great
depth & passion.

Conquer the highest hill together with your love.

Read to each other, share your thoughts,
hopes & dreams.

Believe in each other.

In the power of your love & the strength of your Union.

Be the most trusted person, your best friend & the
person you've search for unknown to you. The universe
answers the call of true love.

Be proud of your love, celebrate it in little ways & big
unexpected ways.

Never give up or give in.

Love is about trying.

Making an effort.

Love is devotional & devotion is prayer.

Make this love so valued you pray for its success & for
it never to end.

Be grateful for this love, for this chance of
divinity & beauty.

Let this love be all it can be.

Let it be so much more than you'd ever imagined or
hope. Discover what love really means when love is built
upon a permanent bond of trust, hope, faith, virtue,
compassion, truth, forgiveness & merkaba.

Love of the light, the love of the body, the worship
of the soul.

T.S.E Beaumont

Call of the Ocean.

True love beckons you, it calls to you, it pulls you
like the ocean.

The great tug of your heart, as it spans the globe
calling you home.

That feeling of being utterly consumed & enraptured
by the divinity of a true soul love, that surrenders
completely, yet never gives up.

Every atom of your being calls to you.

Every nerve ending of your body tingles & twitches
with aliveness & vitality.

Every ounce of light radiates out of your torus field, in
a magnificent arc of beauty.

No this love is not usual or typical or for billions.

It's 1 in 7.6B.

A needle in a haystack, impossible to find or replicate.

It's different for everyone.

So strong it can't be manipulated or destroyed.

It can be attacked, gaslighted, mocked, ridiculed but
it's realness can not be altered or interfered with, its
course is set until the very end.

We all have soulmates, karmic mates, playmates,
unfortunately even hatemates.

But only one true love mate.

Humans are born soft & flowing like the ocean.

Calm and peaceful.

Docile little balls of love, bliss & heavenly divinity.

Of purity & innocence.

As we grow people are very unkind to them, life pokes at them.

People become hardened, jaded & cruel.

People become solid like a rock or a mountain.

Their soft gentleness dissipates, in to displays of mockery and rhino skin behaviour.

Helping a person & changing the world is not about scale.

It's about authenticity.

It's not a numbers game.

It's real living people, with real beating hearts & beautiful brains game.

It doesn't mean publicly showboating your notaries, then becoming a shadow of lies & anger & cruelty.

Authentic behaviour means consistency & not lying.

You change meaningfully, when you truly change yourself in real life in totality.

When you change for the partner you love.

When you grow & evolve & flow together in the open.

The magnificent magnetic pull & resonances which
defies all odds & probability.

The magical feeling of knowing you have found your
divine counterpart & no amount of mud thrown or
quagmire waded through, does it's love or
strength reduce.

Yes love is an ocean & it is soft, smooth and
effervescent.

It flows straight to you where she wraps you
in her arms.

T.S.E Beaumont

Two.

I want a love that is just mine.

No, I do not want to share him with anyone, at all.
Unless, I choose.

Love is universal & we love in a multiplicity of ways.
But romantic love is not, romantic love is only for two.

Three is uncomfortable, jealous, insecure,
manipulative, duplicitous, hateful, envious, boastful,
arrogant, dogmatic, stigmatic, not truthful & just
not true love.

I want to make a jumbled tangled mayhem of
love with him.

I want him to be utterly consume me with his
devotion to me.

Me that's right.

Only me.

Sure sharing is caring.

Threesome are glee some.

But I wanna give me some.

I want to respect him, to have reverence for him.

I want to feel proud & delighted by him.

I don't want a bitchy guy, a bully guy, an abusive guy,
an angry guy or a macho guy.

But to be honest I wouldn't want this in a
woman either.

I want a person who is kind & loving.

Nurturing & evolving.

Not mean & callous, cruel man.

I don't want a mocker or a hater.

A talker or a baiter.

I don't want an egomaniac or a sexmaniac.

I want a man who walks his talk & is honest
completely.

I want a partnership.

A friendship.

A relationship.

A loveship.

A spaceship.

A dreamship.

I want to hold his hand & feel proud of him always.

I want him to know I am his rock & his support.

I want to comfort him when he is weak & scared.

I want him to do the same for me.

I want to be his confident.

His greatest distraction & his greatest inspiration.

In love, there is simply not three.

There is you a me.

There are no third wheels or triangles or hangers on.

There is no vindictive or Machiavellian behaviour.

I want a real man.

I want a true man.

I want my man.

Yes my man.

Not your man.

I want a man, who makes me melt like butter when he looks at me.

I want a man, to hold me tight when we embrace, I want to feel myself collapsing in love, secure in his arms and his kiss.

I want a mental equivalent, who gets life.

Who isn't perfect.

But try's always.

I don't want a quitter.

Someone who gives up the game of life.

I want the last man standing.

I want a man with stamina & perspective.

I want a man that is soft as a marshmallow & as sweet as honey.

I want a gentle loving soulful man, who I
promise to love.

T.S.E Beaumont

Rare.

How rare it is to have someone that truly understands you.

A person whom knows your energy, can interpret your vibration.

The best relationship is one who knows your eyes.

Whom knows that your eyes speak their very own language of truth.

Eyes that speak more truth than words.

The soul of a person is found in the eye.

It's the view out & the view in to the depth of a person.

We seek a person to truly understand us.

To see us.

To feel us.

We want someone to forgive our shortcomings & see there absolute beauty.

We want to be loved & nurtured when we feel sick & pampered with loving adoration.

We want the bad times to be minimised & improved & we need to be cared for deeply.

We want the simplicity of life to overcome our wants.

We want to appreciate the things you can do by merely opening your eyes & looking around.

We want to savour the blissful moments of doing nothing but cuddling.

We want to be read to and told stories of knowledge and surprise.

We want to savour sumptuous meals with each other.

We want to bath in the ocean all day long, then snooze in the hammock til the sun is complete gone.

We want to climb as high as we can and see as far as is possible.

The amazing moments of seeing & doing everything together.

The ecstatic moments of making love all night.

We want a partnership. A romance.

A epic love story.

We want a love that never gives up, always tries and never fails us.

We want a best friend.

An unequivocal and unwavering love to the very end.

T.S.E Beaumont

The Heart.

One glorious kiss on your wondrously gorgeous lips.

The room spins out of control as you fill me with
loving desires & gentle tenderness.

Your love is all I've ever wanted, but never
truly known.

You are such a marvellous enigmatic light of shining
emotion & beauty.

My heart enlarges with each positive word of
affirmation & your voice of wisdom has the most divinely
calm impact on my spirit.

There is no power struggle between us, we lovingly
accept each other.

Your flaws are my favourite thing about you.

I see so much more in you than anybody
could ever see.

You are a creative beacon of light & hope.

You live in your truth & you never hurt
others with words.

You understand language can be hurtful & be
weaponised & it can also heal and cut a person in two.

A love which enables one to completely transform &
transmute, fear and inadequate feelings of despair.

A love like ours is the tiny bird, with the most exquisite
song which you want to protect its uniqueness and
its frailty.

But this love is not frail, it is strong.

I offer you my heart completely.

This heart has loved, it has lost, it has died, it has
known sickness, it has known pain, it has known beauty,
it has known bravery, it has known cruelty, it has known
hate, it has known joy, it has known happiness, it has
known excitement, it has know the full grammut of
earthly emotions since its inception and creation of me.
This heart has felt so many vivid emotions with each
sound it creates. With each divine breath it absorbs the life
force of existence.

This heart makes its own unique music.

It is not a clone or even popular at all. It is special,
unique, one of a kind, not mass produced and for many.
The heart is truly only loved by a few.

This heart never sought many.

This heart has always went in search of the real
truth of life.

It is my sacred heart.

This heart stopped when we met.

It restarted like an electrical current, entirely of it's
own unexpected & unexplainable volition.

The magnificent resonance changed like a quickening.

The final chance it was given to find yours.

This heart loves only you & it's yours if you want it.

T.S.E Beaumont

Spellbound.

My spellbound heart is utterly hypnotised by you.

Holding you in my arms as you float in a haze
of passion.

You are a most delicate creature of exquisite beauty.

Your essence fills my swollen heart with
magical energy.

I watch you intently as your hair falls in a cloud of fine
silken thread around your heart shaped face.

My love for you is immense and expansive.

I feel fiercely protective of you, I want no further harm
to come to you.

I want you to heal & feel safe finally.

I want this love to be all that you need or want.

I want you to feel secure & know that this love is worth
it all and more.

I want to to understand the moment we first met I felt
calm, alive & at peace.

You must know that you enliven my soul with radiant
warmth & deliciousness.

You smell like the sweetness of a dewy flower and
your skin is so dewy, soft & youthful.

Your dimples are the most gorgeous & adorable, they
are beyond indescribably cute.

The way the light hits your luminous eyes which
change colour with your mood, the ocean, the food you
eat, or clothes you wear.

The are a changeble masterpiece of beauty.

The bravery at which you put your heart on display,
you risk all in the name of this love.

Your unwavering trust & belief in me.

You support & listen to every word or perspective.

You objectively share views & ideas to the challenges.

You are divine ray of sunshine on the the cloudy days.
You are the sweet rain that calls on my face.

You are my rainbow after the storm.

You are the cool breeze on a humid day.

You are the lightening that strikes my heart
minute by minute.

You are the air that I breath.

You are the wild temptress ocean of romance.

You are the mountain of strength.

You are the vast green meadow.

You are the wise old tree.

You are the rambling cottage garden.

You are the lush tropical rainforest.

You are the rushing waterfall.

You are the crystal clear stream.

You are the beautiful bird singing.

You are the puppy playing.

You are the pussycat purring.

You are every love song ever written.

You are all the finest words I've ever uttered.

You are the most stunningly beautiful gallery of art.

You are more than any person could see, you are the
one true woman for me.

☛ *T.S.E Beaumont*

Hold Me.

Hold me whilst I surrender.

While I surrender this strength, let me become weak, let me become vulnerable.

Allow me to be softer, to be gentle, to unfold like a beautiful rose, petal by petal, until I have completely unfurled in your love.

Let me not be tough & brazen, let me not be loud & brash.

Let me be ethereal & kind, let me be the true feminine I am meant to be.

Let me not be conformed & conditioned to fight & rage like an old warhorse from hell.

Let the light & air of heavenly grace descend & carry me off in a cloud of safe security & divinity.

Let my sacred femininity rise in the truth of real vulnerability.

Woman are strong, but we need to be gentle, calm, peaceful & loving.

Our greatest gift to our sons is to allow them to cry, to express, to feel & to soften to the poetry that is this life.

The truth of the divinity of this alchemical connection is simple & true.

We all must soften & surrender to the love inside us all.

The feminine nurturing goodness.

The sacred woman inside us all is about this power to peace, to calm, to be truly seen in our authentic truth of our delicate state.

Drop the name calling & patriarchal wand you continue to wave unbeknownst to yourselves.

Abandoned the utter madness of war, strife, & combative hostility.

You are part man & part woman.

To surrender to true love in you & in others, woman must drop their own male tendencies.

Women bleed & they lead, with grace, with compassion, with understanding, with truth, with beautiful looks, with minds of expression & expansive knowledge.

Women are the creators of life & connect deeply with the earth mother they came from, this is the gift we have to offer, that we came from the joy of understanding this connection to all.

So surrender whole & fully to the man you love.

Tell him you are sad, you are afraid, that you need him, that you want him, that you dream of him, tell him you don't want to ever loose him.

But most of all love him, surrender completely & absolutely to the burning love that you feel for him. Submit to your great ego & desire for fame, power and walking on any man, woman or obstacle that cuts through your path.

Live in true, abundance of honesty.

T.S.E Beaumont

Immersion.

I want to immerse myself in your oceanic fountain of love.

To completely surrender to this tumbling, crashing and cascading womb of life.

As I walk into the vast enveloping womb, I wish to be completely and utterly consumed by the force of this feeling.

I stand in the birth canal of this world, the salt watery existence of this life.

The rushing waters of swirling and mixing, building and dancing all over me and glorious delight.

A frothing, bubbling, effervescent concoction of magical alchemical elixir.

I plunge deeper into the vibrant depths of this strong passion, my body is swept into the pool of life with force and feeling.

I am mixing and mingling with ancestral memories and experiences which have been celebrated for millennia.

My body is adorned with the beautiful pleasures of our birthright and natural condition.

I am swept away in swirling universes and galaxies of consciousness.

I feel cleansed, alive and reborn into this moment of purity and energetic release.

My essence floats to new levels and knows no boundaries as it frees from the shackles and limitations, into a wild free place of flight.

T.S.E Beaumont

Dissolve.

When you kiss me my entire form dissolves

In a rush of divine energy.

I'm reduced to a swirling mass of numberless forms
and tingling electrical sensations.

I'm blissfully free, yet completely entangled and
enraptured by this love's expressionism.

You enamour me with your lips, as they search with
complete knowledge and understanding of our love.

Your gaze makes my belly dance in flittering emotional
wonder and in atonement to this time.

My heart fills with poetic reverence, it is completely
filled with divine love and admiration for you my love.

My soul fills with the radiant songs of love and blissful
beauty of heart warming rapture.

Love must be secure in the knowledge that there is no
other truth than ours.

This interwoven story of gorgeous soul filling
loveliness is what we all deeply must know.

Our edges are blurred in the beautiful dancing rhythm
of devotion.

T.S.E Beaumont

Envelope Me.

Envelope me in your love.

Your warmth & compassion elevates my senses to ethereal heights of pleasure.

The strength of your charisma is a cathartic & healing simultaneously.

Your presence is secure & comforting to my soul.

I can tell you all without embarrassment or hesitation.

My deepest fears & worries.

My inadequacies & my shortcomings.

My problems & my mistakes.

My weaknesses & utter vulnerability.

But is not the place I stay.

I merely pass through and expel and integrate the shadow as I travel through to the other side of the spiral.

Life is the lows & the highs.

Truth be told you are not truly living if you have only had a smooth ride.

We are here to learn.

Think about those boat trips, how exciting is it when you hit that big unexpected wave & you pass through the other side.

Life in reality is a beautiful reminder that pain is only temporary, albeit sometimes persistent.

Afterwards, the remnants allow for a beautiful path of knowledge, infinite wisdom learned & earned as a reminder of the journey.

This life is also about the artistry & alluring adventures we experience.

It is important to realise that it is not always the biggest, brightest, most polished & most expensive feat that leads to a life well lived.

Rather life is a tapestry of interwoven delicacies which make ones life whole.

Like the dappled light radiating through the summer leaves, it's the sparkling water on the open seas, it's the intense hues of the vast skies, it's the walking barefoot on the hot sand.

Moments like savouring your favourite ice cream delight on a humid day & eating a mango as the juice drips down your chin.

The warmth of a coffee in your hand as you stroll the wintery streets & it's the leaves that dance around your feet as you rush into the warmth of an art gallery or cosy book store.

The grandest experiences and travels are also amazingly marvellous.

Yet a memorable life is about all of it in its splendours, wonders and awesome goodness.

And it's also how you survived it and survived the challenges and never once gave up, gave in and took the easy escape.

It's how you faced the dragon head on and took charge of your fate

T.S.E Beaumont

Move me.

You move me. You move me to act, to dream, to see, to believe, but mostly to love.

You are the answer to every question, you are the missing piece of the puzzle, you are the jewel in the crown, you are the song of my soul.

You are the swing in my step, the flush in my face, you are the glimmering shimmering shine in my eyes, you are the beat of my heart.

You are the smoothness of my touch, the crinkles around my eyes, the dimples in my smile, the butterflies in my tummy.

You are the swing in my step and the groove in my dance, you are the sultry aroma, you are the soaring delights.

Your gaze sets my heart ablaze and your voice is soothing like a poet. You are the the love I never saw coming, the one that took me by surprise.

You are the one who listened, who learned, who helped, who cared, who tried and who never stopped trying.

You are the gentle touch and the passionate emotion. You are the seeking mind, the loving heart, the strong body and the ecstatic soul.

You are the one that never lied, never tried to hide, that revealed the whole truth, that was open, vulnerable and honest.

You are a scholar and teacher, a king and prince, you are an artist and a scientist, you are an actor and a muse, you are an intellect and a comedian, you are a performer and have your shy blushing ways of honesty and truth.

Your smile is the most beautiful I've ever encountered and your eyes the gentlest and most authentic I have looked into deeply.

You are the kindle, the fire, the flame and bonfire.

You are special beyond belief, unique in every single way, adorable beyond words, sexy beyond belief, you are the one sensation I absolutely can't live without.

T.S.E Beaumont

Tenderness.

The tenderness of your touch is as gentle as your love.

These emotions tickle my senses, like a feather does as
it floats over your skin.

Like the sweet nectar of a luscious peach, which fills
your mouth with delightful bursts of fresh ambrosia.

The rhapsodic dance of wondrous provocative
feelings, which makes my spirit soar & my soul sing.

These playful romantic interludes of musical melodies
& glorious epiphanies of insight which fill me with
marvel & fascination.

Time spent with you fells like seconds, each moment is
draped with such emotional richness & delight.

There is an absolute joy of understanding another, with
such depth & passionate knowledge makes a powerful
bond of consciousness.

Meaningful love which connects you beyond measure
& grows despite all challenges is the love we crave.

To be truly seen for all the wounds experienced in life,
have burned & infused with the light of faith, love & trust.

To be recognised for your kindness & compassion
which reaches to help others, not to hurt them &
ridicule them.

Earning great respect from the trauma which has
shaped your characteristics & calm.

A great love who truly listens & hears every
single word.

Who understands all your gestures & body language,
can interpret the language of your eyes & hear the music
of your soul.

But most of all they understand your silences & they
never stops the good fight.

A love that never gives up on you, doesn't hurt you,
doesn't call you names, does not mock you publicly, that
has nothing but respect & admiration.

A love like this is possible.

A love like this begins with you.

The need, the want, the burning desire to know &
understand someone completely & wholly.

All the complexities & imperfections.

The things that make them weep, the things that make
afraid, the reason the can't sleep, the reason you can't
really eat.

This person knows you completely & the love you
with every single ounce of their existence.

They adore you for your vulnerability which makes
them more giddy with love.

The are in awe of your confidence & how you pick
yourself up & dust yourself of after ever mishap or
fall from grace.

They are your confidant & love you
entirely completely.

T.S.E Beaumont

Your Kiss.

Your kiss sends me straight to the heavens in
calming happiness.

The exquisite feeling of being woken from a deeply
peaceful slumber, with the gentleness of the light quiver
of your lips brushing ever so softly against mine.

I am already in a deeply surrendered blissful state.

The kiss sends a ripple of delicious warmth,
throughout my entire body, as I sleepy stretch and open
my eyes and see your gentle smiling gaze.

A beautiful wave of love courses over me, as we
embrace in loving desire. This feeling of rushing craving
for you fills me with overwhelming passion.

As our kissing becomes more fervent all I see and feel
is you and this divine space. Yearning for this moment,
you completely take control and devour me in unmixed
devotion. Cascades of delight and warmth fill me
completely in a haze of effervescence.

My soul sings with utter contentment, I feel in
complete harmony with you, lying in the protection
of your arms.

T.S.E Beaumont

Climb.

Our love allows you to climb to new heights of reality.

It makes you brave beyond belief & more compassionate in understanding the fundamentals of our earthly condition.

When we are aligned in mind we can understand & contemplate the most extraordinarily magnificent thoughts.

Your mind penetrates mine so fully & completely, that each petal of my existence is known, understood accepted & savoured.

There are no secrets here.

All the shadowy work has surfaced and revealed.

It has been brought into the light of existence of truth through the levels of consciousness, from subconscious to higher self.

True alchemy is turning pain into pleasure.

Turning denial into acceptance.

Turning fear into love.

The artful weaving of musical symposiums, to use these as storytelling telling techniques to build understanding, compassion & empathy.

The emblematic mind can create a viscerally powerful link to the need & desire to triumph over adversity.

It is used as a call to arms to love more, to be more
peaceful in a juxtaposition of frail, yet power
human divinity.

The mind's complex expansiveness must experience a
knowingness, a security & an understanding to be truly
consciously consumed by love.

The heart connection which can not be broken
by another.

The heart that beats as one love & one voice which
knows only the sound of each other's creation.

The soul whom calls to you throughout the day
& the night.

That emblazons in a fiery gust of passion, the soul
connection which pulled us together, from that first
encounter in a mystical & mysterious magnetisms
experienced by few.

Deified & worshipped fully and completely.

Our souls sing the song of our understanding & our
undying love for each other.

These souls are cut from the same source of existence
& can be stretched, torn, injured, break, but will never be
separated or turn away from each other.

The conviction & strength of souls fuels raging passion
& ignites other souls.

The body is a vessel of our love, the last destination.

The one that longs for the pleasure of touch, the sensations you physically give me, the act of letting this love wholly penetrate and consume our human existence.

A longing for consummation.

T.S.E Beaumont

Utopian Mists.

Lying in a sanguine mist of my soul's
utopian happiness.

I lie here thinking of you, needing you, wanting you.

Wanting you so much, for this love to be real and true.

The call and desire of this loves mystical attraction.

The depth, absolutely ferocity and vastness
of this love.

The understanding that their is no other love like this,
or will ever exist, but in this sacred space we have created.

The contemplation that this manifestation is of epic
proportions and of heightened, dramatic theatrical quality.

This love is a waking dream, of all the love stories we
have ever seen and more, because it is unique.

It is ours, it is for you and me.

It is this love that we have shared and created for others
to see, to feel, to touch, to witness, to understand, to
interpret, to harness, to cherish, to enjoy and relish.

The openness and the frailties of being a true and
real person.

The strength and the scorching passion of our souls as
the amplify their authenticity.

As I drift. I drift to you my love.

I travel by air on a whim, a breeze and a gusty zephyr of adoration.

The beauty and the tenacity of this connection is to be revered and respected.

It's stunningly beautiful existence, in its own permanent universe of our creation.

Draping our consciousness like beautiful art in a gallery or a silken robe on the beautiful female body.

Love adorns you completely, fully and entirely.

As it should, filling your cup and overflowing in exuberant happiness and bliss.

T.S.E Beaumont

Sacred Dance.

This is my soul's dance.

As I weave, sculpt and artfully create a living digital
tapestry of my life's expression and experiences.

My life is not straight forward, far from it.

My life is not easy, but there is no mountain I wouldn't
climb to live in absolute truth and reality.

My life was once charmed, money, career, possessions,
travel, awards all the superficialities of the life we all live
and call our own.

I was close to the very pinnacle, when the true
awakening occurred, all goals were attained.

I was awoken to the truth of who I was, the reality of
what we have built and the dismay at the systems we have
created which makes hearts split open, brains collapse,
souls sick and bodies weak.

This dance has been one of fright, flight and freeze in a
perpetual cycle for a significant amount of time.

It has been searing tough and burningly beautiful, as I
have systematically omitted all that is not true or real.

I have cathartically cleansed my career, family, friends.

Some may say it's crazy or a crisis.

I say it's a crisis not to love yourself and protect your
soul essence and the people you love.

In honesty, I am happy with my nearest of kin which only a handful and I realise and savour solitude and peace.

My spirit wants to soar, to sing, to dance, to create and even to sleep.

I do things that feed who I am, that evolutionary path which paves new trails of existence, not reliant on any personal acceptance, but my own.

In truth, I don't care if I'm not liked, not accepted, not popular.

Truth never is.

I'm happy to be real and free and I long for my divine counterpart to share this dance with me across the universe of life.

I have a lot to give, a lot to love and a lot to be. I want this person to truly see the real me.

To bear witness to the pleasures and pains of life.

To authentically and vulnerably exist in the beauty of our planet, to celebrate the magnificent vistas and the glorious skies.

To lovingly resurrect the goodness of the divine partnership which will always be imperfectly perfect go me.

But mostly to see & been seen for the realness of this love of life, this creativity which proliferates in all directions coursing a magically sacred path.

T.S.E Beaumont

The Goddess.

The Goddess is in you, she is in me.

She has the wings of an angel, and burning
fire of a volcano.

She is demure and a temptress.

She is a benevolent being and a brave
warrior of light.

Her words cut with truth, and heal
with gentleness.

She dancings to the beat of her own drum
and the harmonics of the universe.

She communicates with the ocean of our
existence and the breath of our life and reality.

She is tune with frequency all vibrations of
our natural world.

She is a creator of artistry and beauty,
music, images, technology, a lyricist, a
linguist, a painter, sound alchemist.

So tows the order and betweenness of a
evolution and the expansive magisteriums of
our existence.

Divine order is what she seeks, balance,
unity, justice, equality, oneness, peace and
above and beyond all true love.

She is vulnerable and expressive.

Clear and coherent.

She is multifaceted and complex, but also
frustratingly simple and poignant.

She is calm and balanced, but do not push
her over the edge of reason or fairness, as you
will see the truth of all things.

Be honest and share your realness and
feelings and you will earn her
respect and trust.

Listen to her, feel her, touch her, want her,
need her, tantalise her, taste her, give to her,
recurve from her, enrapture her with
all you are.

If you give yourself to her fully, then she
will always love you, believe in you,
care for you.

Protect you.

She will fight with you and alongside you.

She will give you hope and share
your dreams.

She will respond & respect you
beyond words.

You will feel her in your mind talk to you,
in your heart loving you, in your body
calming you, in your soul understanding you.

All conditions will be deciphered and all
unknowns be known.

She will surprise & delight you in flights of
fancy and frivolous feminine desires
& fantasy's.

Her imagination conjures of the grandest
ideas and new pathways of being & living.

Creativity springs in an endless well spring
of prophecy, unique designs & fresh
intelligence.

She celebrates the past, lives in the present
and plans the future.

May you know her, may you see her, may
you fight for her, may you worship her, may
you be her, may you love her.

T.S.E Beaumont

Pure Energy

Out of the rushing womb of water we
came to be.

A woman's very existence is cascading
radiant love.

Born of water and pure primal energy and
alchemical majesty.

A creational woman is in flow with the
universal essence and power of Gaia.

She is voluptuous and soft and
ferocious and strong.

She is demure and coy, but also passionate
and powerful.

A woman is a pure force of nature and
steering beauty.

To truly love a woman, you must know
her completely.

You must gently unfold each petal of her
womanly existence.

Layer upon silken layer of her human divinity,
you must understand and learn her entirely.

You must love her frailties most, you must
nurture these with loving attention.

Her sadness and her weakness will make you
love her more, if the love is real and true.

You will understand and protect her from her
greatest anguished and fears.

You will never ridicule and belittle her, but
rather nurture and support her with care
and kindness.

You will adore her inquisitive mind and her
burning desire to know all things, both how and
why, who, what, when and where.

You'll have empathy with her anxieties and
work to alchemise it together.

You'll chuckle at her bravado and her brazen
attempts to brush away the mishaps and
the challenges.

She'll exhaust you constantly sometimes with
her buzzing and busy nature and make you smile
with amusement and weary bliss.

You'll stay up late together, talking all night
underneath the glimmering moon, thinking about
everything and anything worth contemplating.

The blissful mornings together with sleepy
eyes, bedhead and bare bodies will warm your
heart and fill you with absolute delight.

You will relish time alone most of all.

You will savour and feel exhilarating fulfilled
adventuring whether I'd be travelling, exploring,
hiking or swimming.

You will dive into all artistic pursuits and
savour art, the music, film, theatre, literature all
experiences and expressions.

Bathing at home or in the sea will have
enrapturing happiness of togetherness.

Making love and letting love make you in all
the ways, everyday.

Together you will love like no other.

A brave beautiful and unstoppable force made
for each other.

T.S.E Beaumont

Carry

Sometimes in life we can no longer
walk alone.

Sometimes we need the one we love,
to carry us.

To carry the pain, the burden, the trauma.

We want the person we love to fight the
demon with us.

To tell people it is not ok to do this to the
person you love, let alone any human being.

We need to disrupt & explode the system.

There is combination of pain & pleasure that
are needed to change this world.

When you stand alone in your truth, people
stone you with hate & vitriol.

People do not lovingly embrace you.

In this life people say they love you but they
are more inclined to hurt you through jealousy,
hatred & envy.

There is an innate insidious darkness which
afflicts the human race.

People would rather spiritual bypass, than
become vulnerable to the truth of the real human
condition & the endless suffering for people
whom tell the truth.

It is apparent, people can not handle the truth,
in a world where we are trained to superficially
glide through life.

True life & love is pain and suffering, it is
also beauty & divine grace.

Real love springs from a deep well of
understanding & a desire to heal at a deal
soul level.

The shadow creates the brilliance and
blinding light of persons soul.

The depth of the scars allow more beautiful
light to radiate.

People crucify human beings for standing up
for their rights.

They drag them through mud, processes &
systems design to break the human spirit and
destroy the human soul.

The souls that fight injustice & oppression
are the most powerful in existence.

The passion, exhuburance, gusto &
conviction they stand in propels this decaying
human race forward to new unprecedented
levels of consciousness and awareness.

Life is much more than just flowers & trees.

Humans are connected to the super
consciousness of planet.

We have the unparalleled ability to think,
feel, do, see & create like no other.

We also have the ability to change systems,
infrastructure and brokenness which destroys
people & lives with unbelievable cruelty.

So to the woman or man who fight for truth
and justice, support them, get behind them.

For goodness sake carry them.

If you don't understand, try, learn empathy.

Truly feel.

T.S.E Beaumont

Embrace.

When we embrace, your protection surrounds me in
the glorious warmth of adoring tenderness.

Everything fades to just you, your heavenly touch and
your presence infuses my every sense.

The sweetest kiss of love, fills me with tingling
delights which melt like fairy floss.

The effervescent tickles, which cover my skin make
me filled with delighted happiness.

To be in your arms is the most exquisitely rapturous
sensation and makes my tummy flitter, and flutter like a
butterfly dancing in the wind.

The waft of classical music permeates through the air
and soundscapes our environment, it is a soothing
melodic array of wondrous emotions.

The wind gently blows around us and plays with our
hair and our garments, as we cling to this loving moment
and embrace.

When I look at your eyes, I see the light of your soul,
dance and flicker in your eyes in luminous peace.

The afternoon sun fills us with a golden glow and
radiant feeling of glimmering intensity.

Each moment we spend together is so precious
and special.

You fill my heart with such intense feelings of love
and reverence.

I am grateful for my soul's birth and for the ability to connect so deeply with the other.

The deep resonance and magnetism between us, even in silence is the most powerful and potent nectar.

I feel the gaze of others watching our carefree love and the smiling acknowledgement of respect fills our surroundings.

Love not only fills you up, it fills others up.

True open love gives others something to hope for, to strive for, not to critique and criticise.

Ultimately, love is pure acceptance of who you are, it is understanding, tolerant, forgiving and filled with grace.

Love wants only the very best for you, love wants to see you win.

Love wants to share the feeling and radiant pleasure outwardly with the world.

The true heart of love is your core existence.

The feelings of love emanate from the creation source of love.

The heart and soul of a woman and a man in this sacred dance of love everlasting.

T.S.E Beaumont

Cocoon.

Make me a cocoon of our love.

Weave your spell of enchantment around this vessel.

Fill me completely with the divinity of your protection.

Enrapturing beauty of this love that is ever expanding
like the universe, yet safe and warm like the womb of life.

Hold me in your arms with such strength and
gentle tenderness.

Carry this love to new height of
understanding and care.

Make the clouds blush in astonishment of the power
and majesty of this loves passion.

Make the sun explode in delight with the burning
desire to shield and defend.

Make the clouds dancing in rushing gusts of air.

Make the sky cry in the blissful beauty and reverence.

Make the earth shake and rumble in
thunderous applause.

May this love be unstoppable and true.

May this love never falter or waiver.

May the essence of our love infuse others souls with
hope, faith and truth.

In the end this love is all there is.

Love beyond measure or boundaries.

There no rules or conventions, guides and truths.

But all love is unique and special and different for all.

But the love I want is the highest order of all.

One that never dies.

Just this splendid rapturous truth of all this love is, and will continue to become for evermore and eternity.

T.S.E Beaumont

Breathtaking.

Life should take you breath away.

These little moments of divine, breathlessness.

When you become overwhelmed with the beauty of a
sensation or moment.

Moments like breathtaking sunrises and sunsets, that
also fill you with exquisite vitality and serenity at
the same time.

Moments like that accidental gentle brush of your
lovers skin next yours which makes you skin, which
makes you respond in rippling happiness.

Moments like the sweet smell of the man you love
filling your nostrils with his heavenly aroma.

Moments like the gentle kissing which becomes deep,
more passionate and searching.

Moments like the fluttering butterflies which fill your
tummy when he looks at you that special way, which
makes you gasp with delight and swoon with loving
recognition.

Moments that take your breath away are what life is all
about, because when breath returns, so too is the
willingness to encounter more breathlessly beautiful
moments which make you aware of your humanity, yet
filled with pure divinity and infinite love.

✍ T.S.E Beaumont

Women.

There are times in life when a women, needs to be protected. Fiercely needed and fiercely loved.

To be wrapped in the security of loving and faithful arms.

To be held and know that she is safe and everything is alright.

To be reassured that you will get through the endless suffering and challenges.

To know that you are not fighting in vane, that it a good fight.

A worthwhile fight.

A fight that has a reason and a cause.

A women is many different things, in many different ways, on many different days.

A woman is a divine mother and part of the universal circle of life.

A woman is a goddess and a galactic being of both destruction and creational source and power.

A woman is an ascended master of the solar system and both a muse and a demon.

A woman is a spiritual leader who cascades sacred knowledge and future visionary pathways from a crowning leadership source.

A woman is an oracle and seer and has an inner
knowing of all things past, present and future which she
gleans from intuitional strength.

A woman is a wise woman who has seen and knows
and does, she walks her talk.

A woman is healer, a nurse, a medicine woman, a
midwife with the skills to lovingly fix what has
been broken.

A woman is a nurturing mother who leads with her
heart and is always loving and true, kind and
compassionate.

A woman is a magician, a nun, a witch, a worshipper,
as she speaks she creates all things in a sweeping gesture.

A woman is a tantric lover, she is both a wife and a
whore, a woman possesses the gift of sensuality and
erotic love simultaneously.

A woman is an Amazon warrior, a fighter of the world
and a protector of truth and justice.

A woman is a Mother Earth, she is the source of all life
and creator of the human race.

And despite all these gifts and abilities, women need to
be protected and defended by each other and by men.

Because without women we simply do not exist.

To all these women you are loved.

You are needed, you are respected.

You are, woman.

T.S.E Beaumont

Utter Devotion.

I love you with utter devotion and completely.

I worship every single element of the experiences that
have made you, you.

I accept you, for who you are completely and
without question.

I see your weaknesses, these so called flaws, but I find
these so beautiful and they only make me love
you even more.

The pain and suffering that often shapes people, is in
fact that which makes them so special and unique.

I respect and adore your honesty and the gorgeous way
your soul speaks to mine in absolute truth.

This truth is beauty, this beauty is honesty, this
love is rare.

But it need not be.

We all have the potential to care with such depth and
ferocity if we only live in truth and be unafraid of who we
are and what has shaped us.

By being really you, you open the path for others to
do the same.

The vulnerability of our love is a rare covenant, it is a
true treasure and a testament to its strength
and endurance.

There is power in gentleness and sensitivity, when true
love is allowed to flourish.

The way you touch my essence, you fill me with so
much emotion, warmth and unbridled loyalty.

You are the one who makes me feel, the one who
brings me comfort and makes me feel not so alone.

The way you listen to me, to every single thing and
care for all the tiny details.

You always touch me without touching me, because
you truly see me, as I truly see you.

Whenever you caress me I am so alive and enraptured
by your gaze.

The confidence and safety this love provides make me
know I can face anything, because your love won't
waiver, it will only grow and swell.

This love makes me surrender to you wholly.

It is true people are imperfect, but you are
perfect for me.

T.S.E Beaumont

Know Me.

I want my lover to know me.

To know every inch of my skin.

I want him to index every single freckle with his
finger tip.

I want him to sooth and kiss every scar with loving
tenderness.

I want to feel his body melt into mine like a hand into a
velvet glove.

I want his scent to fill my sense with his
warm manliness.

I want us to discover each other over and over and
over again.

I want to lie in each other's arms in bliss and harmony.

I want to feel that unrestrained urge to touch
each other.

I want my stomach to dive into the abyss when you
look at me and then soar back to the sky.

I want to feel weak with true love of the soul.

I want the world to melt from view and all I see is you.

I want the love of mind to be filled with delicious deep
meaningful meanderings.

I want to be with the man that chooses me.

I want to choose only him.

I want to be lovingly kind, honestly faithful and scrupulously truthful.

I want this love to see me.

To know me.

To understand me.

To listen to me.

To hear me.

To just love me.

T.S.E Beaumont

Burning Need, Want and Desires.

Needs and wants, hopes and desires are all
the same to me.

I wish upon a star that my wishes will be real
and true......

I see you,

I want to be seen.

You are my love,

I want to be loved.

You are my beginning,

I want to be your beginning.

You are my ending,

I want to be your ending.

I long for you to be here by my side,

I want you to long and need me to be
by your side.

I need to be physically comforted,

I want to be physically comforted

I need you to hold me, I want you to hold me.

I need to be loved, I want to be loved.

I need to be supported, I want to
be supported.

I need protection, I want protection.

I need to be kissed, I want to be kissed.

I need to be cuddled, I want to be cuddled.

I need to be felt, I want to be felt.

I need to be savoured, I want to be tasted

I need you to make love to me, I want you to
make love to me.

I need to be with you, I want to be with you.

I want to share this life and this love I will
wait to find the right soul.

This life is short, I've made too many
mistakes and frivolous decisions in love and
next time I need and want it to be right to last, to
grow, to evolve, to be all consuming
and to be real.

I need and want to create on scale and I need
and want a man to share my hopes,
dreams and vision.

I need, want and deserve respect.

I need, want and deserve honor of my path of
healing from all kinds of trauma. Not meanness,
not cruelty, not anger, not lies.

Just the truth.

I need someone to be kind and I really want
someone to be kind.

I need and want to believe that there is a
compassionate soul.

I need and want to believe that there is real
love and not fashion faux fraud.

I need and want to be loved unconditionally
and with vigour.

I need and want to live as me in my bare truth
and honesty.

To just be needed, wanted, loved and desired
for all my darknesses and all my light.

T.S.E Beaumont

I Love You

I love you without question.

I love you, without truly knowing the real reason why.

I love you beyond any kind of understanding or comprehension.

I love you when you are happy and smiling.

I love you when you are sad and crying.

I love you when you are zany and silly.

I love you when you are mad and stormy.

I love you when I think it is impossible to love another more.

This love of ours keeps growing, expanding & surprises me evermore.

I love when we sit & you read to me from all your magnificent books.

I love it when we sleep in & snuggle deep within the warmth of the bed.

I love it when we walk, that coldness on our noses and cheeks, but warmth upon our heads.

I love the heat of our coffees shared as we walk down the street & breeze blows around us.

I love admiring the beautiful art with you, as much as peering at beautiful couples and families filled with love, like we have found too.

I love it when I catch you gazing at me & the butterflies
fill my stomach.

I even love just cuddling with you, watching films,
just you & me.

I love the deep immersion in gorgeous hot
bubble baths.

I love the way the sunlights shines & kisses your face.

I love the way the wind dances & plays in your hair.

I love your big beaming smile & raucous laughter.

I love your wild gesticulations, your amazing thoughts
& feelings.

I love your doubts, worries, the fear & pain.

I love your deep beautiful eyes which are burning
pools of love.

I love your gorgeous skin & the way you smell
so delicious.

I love holding your hand & feeling your energy course
through my veins.

I love the way you touch me with such
tenderness & grace.

I love the way you kiss me & leave the biggest smile
upon my mouth.

I love watching you sleeping, the peace written
over your face.

I love the way you try so hard at everything you do & how you are constantly improving & striving for more.

I love the way you've evolved & have grown more comfortable with who you are.

I love the way you sing, dance & express yourself.

I love the way you love me.

There is nobody but you.

All the amazingly beautiful things that you do.

I love you, I just love you.

I honestly do.

T.S.E Beaumont

Devotion

I love you with utter devotion and completely.

I worship every single element of the experiences that
have made you, you.

I accept you, for who you are completely and
without question.

I see your weaknesses, these so called flaws, but I find
these so beautiful and they only make me love
you even more.

The pain and suffering that often shapes people, is in
fact that which makes them so special and unique.

I respect and adore your honesty and the gorgeous way
your soul speaks to mine in absolute truth.

This truth is beauty, this beauty is honesty, this
love is rare.

But it need not be.

We all have the potential to care with such depth and
ferocity if we only live in truth and be unafraid of who we
are and what has shaped us.

By being really you, you open the path for others to
do the same.

The vulnerability of our love is a rare covenant, it is a
true treasure and a testament to its strength
and endurance.

There is power in gentleness and sensitivity, when true
love is allowed to flourish.

The way you touch my essence, you fill me with so
much emotion, warmth and unbridled loyalty.

You are the one who makes me feel, the one who
brings me comfort and makes me feel not so alone.

The way you listen to me, to every single thing and
care for all the tiny details.

You always touch me without touching me, because
you truly see me, as I truly see you.

Whenever you caress me I am so alive and enraptured
by your gaze.

The confidence and safety this love provides makes me
know I can face anything, because your love won't
waiver, it will only grow and swell.

This love makes me surrender to you wholly.

It is true people are imperfect, but you are
perfect for me.

T.S.E Beaumont

Held

I want to be held.

I want to be in your arms and
fearlessly protected.

I want you to keep me warm and safe.

I want you to as fiercely protect me, as
you love me.

I want to be cradled.

I want the physical warmth of you to
infuse my skin.

I want to know you, to feel you, to be with you.

I want you to treat me with respect and care.

I want you to need and want me.

I want you to like and love me.

I want you to respect and value me.

I want to be your best friend and your
confidante.

I want you to be my sounding board and guru.

I want to let you love me, to show me how true
love feels.

I want to surrender to this love, wholly
and completely.

I want to make love and let the love make me.

I want to be devoured and consumed entirely.

I want to be enraptured and in bliss.

I want to lie spent in your arms in a silken
cloud of peace.

I want you. Just you.

I want this love.

I want us.

I just want us.

T.S.E Beaumont

Womb

True love is like the womb of a woman.

It is safe, cosy, enveloping and gentle.

Love cocoons you, it protects you, it keeps you safe.

It is vulnerable and naked in its real truth.

It cloaks you in its warmth and security.

It is the source of divinity and creation of life.

So too it is a force to be reckoned with if true and real.

It is powerful, strong and magnificent.

It is nurturing, tender and soft.

It wraps you in silken gentleness and loves you
unconditionally to peace.

All our lives we look for a love and place such as this.

That loves us throughout our challenges, stretching and growth.

That is our greatest cheerleader, supporter and confidante.

That loves our weakness to strength and resilience and triumph.

That enhances and expands us beyond our earthly capabilities
and beliefs.

Love is like the womb, the womb of a woman and also the womb
of our existence.

Mother Earth.

T.S.E Beaumont

Knowing

I want my lover to know me. To know every
inch of my skin.

I want him to index every single freckle with
his finger tip.

I want him to soothe and kiss every scar with
loving tenderness.

I want to feel his body melt into mine like a hand into a
velvet glove.

I want his scent to fill my senses with his
warm manliness.

I want us to discover each other over and over and
over again.

I want to lie in each other's arms in bliss and harmony.

I want to feel that unrestrained urge to
touch each other.

I want my stomach to dive into the abyss when you
look at me and then soar back to the sky.

I want to feel weak with true love of the soul.

I want the world to melt from view and all I see is you.

I want the love of mind to be filled with delicious deep
meaningful meanderings.

I want to be with the man that chooses me.

I want to choose only him.

I want to be lovingly kind, honestly faithful and scrupulously truthful.

I want this love to see me.

To know me.

To understand me.

To listen to me.

To hear me.

To just love me.

T.S.E Beaumont

The Gaze

The intensity of your gaze makes my heart fill with
loving warmth.

My tummy fills with fluttering butterflies without even
being touched.

This dance began long before we even undressed.

The heavenly scent of your manly aroma
fills my senses.

I am so awakened to all that you are.

The divinity of this moment is vulnerable and fluidity.

I want to feel you enter my heart and never
lose this gaze.

I'm filled with so much burning pleasure that I can no
longer hold your gaze.

In this haze of passion I completely let go and submit
to your control in ecstatic surrender.

T.S.E Beaumont

In the darkness, your love surrounds me like a soft velvet cloak.

My senses are completely filled and alive.

The sensuality of your touch makes my heart calm and relax into your loving presence.

I feel alive and revitalised, you awaken all that I am and all that I will be.

This evolution of soul is the journey of life.

To live in truth and realness and in harmony with source and our true burning essence.

You electrify me, your gaze, your touch, your breath, your voice, your energy fills me beyond any earthly description.

The purification of our chakras and the release of the divine nectar of sweet Amrita.

In this sacred moment I am empowered and embodied.

This magical moment of consciousness and divinity.

T.S.E Beaumont

The Music of Love

The music fills my senses with warmth and peace.

As I lie quietly in the dark, absorbing all the harmonic beauty of this moment.

I drift away from my body into an ethereal place and state of being beyond the earthly realm of existence.

I feel tingles surface and warmth drift up from the tips of my toes, slowly rising to my root chakra and stay's there ready to engage.

As the warmth spreads throughout my body, a sense of weight also emerges as my body engages in a heightened state of consciousness and self awareness of the other.

My core being is aligned and ready to uncoil to its full vibrant capacity and elated state of being.

I let go completely and let the feelings wash over me and completely engulf me in a deep state of peace, comfort and heavenly relaxation.

I slowly witness the energy rise through the levels, as my sense of release climbs, escalates and wants to be released in ecstatic surrender.

Your presence embodies me and envelopes me in loving bliss and cascading release and shaking ecstasy.

T.S.E Beaumont

Alchemical Fire.

There is nothing more I want than to be in your
arms. To feel the absolute safety and protection
of your love.

To feel your skin against mine, close, soft,
smooth and warm.

To inhale the scent of your body, the essence of
your existence.

To feel glorious sultriness waft over me as the
glow of love tinges my vision. A feeling that is
better than ecstasy.

When you gaze at me I feel weakened in the
most deliciously rare way.

The sound of your voice reverberates through
my soul in the most soothing way.

This heavenly tenderness and love I feel for
you courses through all that I am, my heart,
mind,body and soul.

Butterflies of emotions fluttering inside me in
an untamed love which only grows and develops.

The longer we are apart the more the desire
deepens and strengthens. I never knew love could
feel like this.

When your lips gently brush mine with your
luscious soft lips the world fades from view and I

am lost in a swirling haze of deep love and
volcanic passion.

It doesn't matter where we are, as long as we
are together.

This love is an alchemical fire of the soul.
Constantly combusting and enhancing to new
levels of awareness.

We are filled with divine enchanting moments
and memories which are for us to savour for all
of eternity.

T.S.E Beaumont

Moments

Moments with just you and I keep me absorbed and at peace.

The beautiful serenity and comfort that exists in the betweenness.

Your presence alayes all my fears and fills me with dreamy happiness.

Your loving gaze enchants my heart, mind, body and soul.

These heavenly days and nights we spend with each other in rapturous pleasure.

In these moments we want for nothing.

Shielded in the protection of each other's loving arms.

Meaningful meanderings filled with exquisite depth of understanding.

I am so sensitive to your touch and your gaze.

A mere gentle brush of touch fills me up with so much love and bliss.

And still when you kiss me the warmth of your lips fills me with absolute devotion.

The tenderness and intimacy we share is so deep and filled with divinity.

The gaze of your eyes fills me with a radiant warmth, which makes me glow with yearning.

These moments with you are what life is all about, the essence of consciousness and true love.

T.S.E Beaumont

The Partnership.

Love is a partnership.

It's interwoven souls, in a tender dance.

It's two hands held tightly, in unwavering support and
acceptance. It's lips locked in a sensual kiss, of
adoration and bliss.

It is the mystery of life. The answer to the riddle, the
solution to the puzzle which gives existence meaning.

The antidote to despair, the reason to believe in a
higher purpose and in God. It's the spring in your step,
and the groove in your glide.

It's the warmth in your heart, and the butterflies in your
tummy. It's the sleepless nights and the sleepy daze days.

It's the warm summer breeze and the cool
twilight haze.

It's the well loved book and the music that makes your
skin quiver and feel.

It's the warm fresh towels, on a cold winter's day and
the smooth cotton sheet on a summer night.

It's the succulent mango which drips off your chin and
the sweetest of strawberries which perfume your skin.

It never gives up, it never gives in.

It's your rock of strength and a shining beacon. Love is
endless and vast and never ending. Infinitely, infinite,
truly never ending.

T.S.E Beaumont

Loves Strength and Armour.

Love is your absolute strength & armour, it
makes you feel invincible.

It is your weakness, & your most honest
vulnerability.

It is wild like a thunderous storm & lovingly
laps, like the sea on a calm day.

It is the strength of a fortress & has the
tenderness of a rose.

Love supports your pains, wants you to heal
& it nurtures your insecurities, with kindness
and compassion.

Love touches your heart, mind, body & soul.

It constantly fills you to overflowing
abundance & everlasting bliss.

Love fills you with effervescent & joy.

It nourishes you in peaceful cascades of
enchantment.

Heavenly moments surround a couple who
are truly in love, it is a frequency
vibrational alignment.

True love is full of wonder and has a
comfortable security, ease & honesty.

My love wants to know me for my true
essence and my reality as a woman.

To be truly known for my loud but quiet
confidence and my humble girly shyness &
nagging self doubt.

Often, I don't think I'm really good enough.

Even though I try so hard to be better each &
every single day.

I realise I don't know it all, done it all,
seen it all.

But I do want to learn more, see more, be
more and feel more.

Some may think that I am vain.

I'm just trying to be real and be
acknowledged for my existence.

Mean spirited people, anger & psychic
attacks hurt my soul & my heart.

It surprises me when I get a compliment and
fills me with unexpected happiness.

I want him to know even if I'm doing a good
job, I think that I'm not.

I want him to know I am sensitive & very
aware & consciousness but not of my
own ability.

Yes I have lived & I have learned and
achieved, but I feel I could do much more &
much better.

I want him to know I was once married to an unkind man, my lack of awareness in this decision haunts me still, to this very day.

I want him to know I so desperately want to protect my children from further harm & I want him to be the best role model for them to look up to and talk too.

I want him to know I'm good at hiding my pain, but it shows in my eyes.

I want to share & feel my way through life.

Living & loving & creating

I want true, lasting love with a person that truly loves only me & is my partner.

T.S.E Beaumont

This Dance.

This is our dance.

Our ecstatic dance of love.

The sacredness of our journey.

The divinity of this encounter.

Our bodies move in unison and harmony.

A dance of oneness and unity.

A supreme honesty and exquisite transparency.

Your touch sends beautiful ripples of loving adoration
throughout my existence.

We are synchronised and together in the beauty of
this moment.

Swirling touch and graceful musical melodies.

Our bodies meld and glide in glorious loving surrender.

This love is all consuming and expansive.

It is vast and otherworldly.

This love is what life is about.

It is the essence of creational power.

T.S.E Beaumont

Forcefield.

Your love is a protective forcefield.

With you I feel safe, heard, witnessed
and understood.

To live a vulnerable and open existence,
requires absolute truth, authenticity and realness.

Your love is of supreme kindness and care.

You are never cruel or toxic.

You are never spiteful or mean.

You do not exact revenge or dictate.

You do not impose patriarchal or matriarchal
dogma upon me.

You are open and full of love and
supreme compassion.

You listen to me and you understand me fully.

You want to learn, you want to understand, you
want to grow together.

Although you need your space, you never leave
my heart, body and soul.

You whisper sweetest thoughts and gentle
poetry through my essence.

The divinity of your caress leaves heavenly
prints of love and tingles of rapture.

To be understood by someone beyond measure
of definition, is the most beautiful
feeling to receive.

To love someone with every ounce of your
existence a most precious gift to be savoured and
treasured for all of eternity.

This kind of love is peace itself.

T.S.E Beaumont

The Wilderness of Our Love.

Pour your love into me.

Shower me completely with heavenly kisses from your
luscious mouth.

Baptise me in the waters of your love.

Enliven my soul and make it float in dreamscapes of
watery bliss.

The tenderness of your touch fills me with such
serenity, peace and calmness.

The water of our love in the wilderness of our earth.

Adorn my body with your love as I surrender
completely to you.

The divine splendour of complete immersion in the
natural world, we are one with each other and our entire
surroundings.

Fill me with your light and glorious rapture of this
sacred dance.

T.S.E Beaumont

Bare.

Strip me back bare. To all I am.

To all you are.

To the pure essence of our love.

The divine nectar or our naked beginnings.
Vulnerable and real.

Honest and true. Giving and loving. Open
and expressive.

Imaginative and evocative.

Seduce my mind with your poetry and my body with
your touch. Consummate this longing with the splendours
of true love.

Pour your soul into mine and commingle in heavenly
states of ecstasy and bliss.

T.S.E Beaumont

Ocean Woman.

Some women are like the ocean.

They are wild and passionate and open with
their primal sexual essence.

Their bodies are temples to be explored,
worshipped and adored.

These women are full of sacred wisdom and
ancient sexual knowledge.

Their very existence is a blessing
and a miracle.

They are temptresses of divinity and
searingly beautiful love and artistry.

A woman's body is a work of art to be
worshipped and adored completely.

Each undulating curve and smooth rounded
voluptuousness element of a true
women's form.

We are not girls, we are goddesses and
bearers of life and creativity and divine vessels
for self expression.

The earthly rawness of what being a woman
is all about.

We are in dialogue with the elements of our
universe, we express these completely and fully.

We are smooth and flowing, not rushed, not
uptight and stiff and jerky.

We know our bodies, we listen to them and
have deep communion with our desires and
inner source.

We flow in unison to the harmonics of life in
an effortless unification.

T.S.E Beaumont

Swirling Energies.

When you enter me I come alive.

We are a beautiful swirling mass of energies.

This feeling is surrounding me and is also inside me.

Everything is heightened and amplified, my skin is so
sensitive to your every touch.

The sound of your breath in delirious pleasure
consumes me and enhances this moment.

The wild pleasure of ecstasy as we soar to new
heights of love.

As I close my eyes I am driven further into a visceral
light show of epic proportions as our energy fields merge,
combine and explode in wonderment.

Our bodies want to take flight in divine pleasure, as we
shake from head to toe in strong vibrating release of
orgasmic pleasure and pure bliss.

T.S.E Beaumont

Me.

Take me.

Tantalise me.

Touch me.

Tease me.

Stroke me.

Taste me.

Enter me.

Fill me.

Feed me.

Devour me.

Soar with me.

Explode with me.

T.S.E Beaumont

Force of Nature.

Emblazoned by love, deeper than earth's core.

Vaster than the expansion of the universe.

This love is a force of nature itself.

It is both destructive and also creative.

It is a supreme healing force of unknown capacity.

This love is enveloping and also freeing.

This love shines with passion and pours with pain.

This love understands all the gradients of life and
also existence.

This love is endless and abundant.

A love that wants to consume and devour me whole.

Desirous of beauty and grace and carnal pleasure.

Exploring the most titillating beginnings to the most
roaringly erotic completion.

A hunger and a desirous wanton need for consumption
and exaltation.

A love that doesn't conquer, instead a love that
evolves, soars and becomes ecstatic states to being
and existence.

This love is in all of us, pure and true and waiting for
ignition and divine birthing of our souls true vaporous
heady truth.

T.S.E Beaumont

Closer.

Come closer.

Come so close that there is no separation between us.

Ignite my body with your sensuous touch.

Melt into me and consume me entirely.

Become one whole being with me.

Feel the sensations beyond the literal.

Swell and grow slowly to great heights of ecstasy
and release.

Absorb this glorious soul love, in the rich technicolor
vibrant hues of its existence.

Be more than you ever were before, expand your
consciousness to the brightest levels of awareness.

Let this divine passion consume our existence in
etheric realms of bliss and splendour.

Fly me to the sky, watch us soar in waves of love and
sonic lights of radiance.

Create with Me.

Create with me.

Create with me a beautiful rhythmical masterpiece
of our love.

Strip your soul back bare.

Completely and utterly vulnerable for the entire
world to see.

Unclothe who you are and become truly naked in this
moment which is eternal.

Join with me in this dance of love.

Bodies collide and hearts explode.

Skin slides and minds soar.

A tangled glorious creation of love, lust and passion.

Fuel my fire and fan the flames of true love's course.

Emerge and embody the wantonly beautiful feeling we
have together.

The gravity of this moment is so intense.

An alchemical fire which burns and combusts in a
magnificent storm of powerful release and searingly
wondrous ecstasy.

Hold me close.

Collapse into me where you belong.

I love you.

All of Me.

I want you to take me.

All of me.

I don't want you to leave a part of
me untouched.

I want your soul to fill me and completely
overflow in our glorious love making.

I want you as close as you can get and as
deep as you can hide.

I want you to fill my challis to the brink of
bursting with ecstasy and then stop.

I want you to hold there, in stillness and
look at my eyes, to feel me, all the soft curves
as inner folds.

To understand the sacred space where you
are being held.

To savour and feel this divine connection
of consciousness and eternal loving embrace.

I want you to absorb every single sensuous
curve and the silken delicate smoothness of
my flowering beauty.

I want you to be slow and so gentle and
drink in every motion and every divine touch.

I want you to really feel where you are.

To understand how beautiful this love is.

I want you to plunge deeper into my
velvety depth and flowering womanhood, to
welcome your powerful and magnetic
strength as it travels into the universe of life.

I want you to feel everything with heavenly
sensuous care.

I want you to feel the warmth and welcome
and enveloping love.

I want to heighten this moment and
experience, take every moment slow, until we
explode in unity together.

You Read Me.

Your smoothness and hardness is irresistible to me.

You tantalise and gently caresses my womanly essence
to new heights of delight and ecstasy .

Your strength and manly form fills me with warmth
and pleasure.

I adore it when you take control, you sense exactly
what I am feeling and you respond with deft grace and
sensual charisma.

You read my body like a very well loved book and
know exactly what it is telling you to do next.

You've indexed ever single part of me, from my crown
to tips of my toes

A touch of the skin, a flicker in the eye, a gentle
sigh or moan.

You respond with knowingness and divine care.

My body luxuriates in your presence and responds
with each movement.

Our love grows and swells, rises and flows to a place of
beauty and heavenly states of blissful being.

You pour your love into me with unending devotion
and worship and my temple responds to your Godly
divinity and our soaring states of illuminations and
states of being.

Enveloping Love.

Let your love envelope me.

Let it embrace me completely.

Allow me to be carried away to states of blissful
comfort and safety.

Let us float in this cloud of love and consciousness.

Drifting through all the passing emotions and
sensations and shivers of ecstasy.

Love me beyond measure and beyond reason.

Love me in my realness and completeness
as I love you.

Forging progressively our bond which has unbreakable
strength and unbridled passionate love.

Feel me so completely, every single part of me, allow
the waves of emotions to take control and soar to new
heights of loving.

Let this love be a safe harbour and a temple of
supreme pleasure.

Together we are unstoppable and we rise like the
Phoenix illuminating the sky in burning glory.

True Loves Burn.

We are burning embers of the brightest star.

Our love burns brighter than any fire.

When you touch me I explode with heat of our divinity.

This energy alchemises in a storm of spiralling waves
of heat fuelled chemistry.

You fill me with such extreme passion and burning
desire which builds beyond volcanic proportions.

This love is earth shaking, body quaking
glorious magic.

Eternity.

In this moment we are eternal. Time stands still.

The sky explodes in blind light.

This love is bigger and more magnificent than
the heavens.

This love is healing, loving, nurturing and fulfilling.

This love is a binding and powerful force which makes
you believe in yourself beyond any comparison.

Gives you the ability to achieve anything you manifest
and do make life imbued deeply by the rich tapestry of
lives divine splendour and beauty.

This love knows no bounds and is eternal and beyond
any earthly description.

This love is an alchemical source of creation
and divinity.

This love commingles with spirit and universe in a
harmonious symphonic loving embrace.

This love dances and dazzles and shines brighter
than any star.

This love is immortalised.

This love is consciousness personified.

Breathe.

Breathe me in, every intoxicating moment we
have together.

Feel my energy radiate, it's burning deep warmth and
loving heat.

Kiss me with such divine passion that you send tingles
coursing throughout my body. Fill me with your essence,
make me understand the truth of this love.

Show me what no other man could ever show me.

Inhale this moment, infuse your body with me, merge
and commingle in soaring states of blissful ecstasy.

Love me in wisdom, in truth, in beauty, in
perpetual motion.

This moment of love never ending, always building,
always growing, always becoming more beautiful with
each passing encounter.

This love is an unstoppable force, it only becomes
more powerful and magnificent with time. This love is an
evolutionary force of alchemical transformation.

This love is always different and always exquisitely
serenely beautiful.

This love kisses you in all the achingly painful places
and heals them with such gentle loving
tenderness and care.

This love is life giving and creational.

This love grows and swells in its abundance to something magical which can be harnessed, spread, shared and magnified to an infinite scale.

This love is we. You and me. Forever in love.

When you first touch me I feel the electricity course from your finger tips onto my skin, my nerve endings tingle with delight.

As we sit naked on the darkened shore the cosmos surrounds us, and time stands still.

We are encompassed by nature completely, as the magnetism of earth and in this moment our love flows freely though-out our bodies and into our natural surroundings.

Each divine touch creates gentle waves of euphoria between us which are building deeply and consciously within our bodies.

Ethereal Love Light.

I feel my body floating in golden waves of ethereal
light and energy, as we worship each other completely,
with unmistakable prayer like passion.

The stars twinkle above us in the new moon light and
the ocean glimmers, glistens and laps gently at our feet.

We are so immersed in each other, cocooned in this
natural deserted environment only for us.

This encounter of love is a sensory heavenly moment
of bliss, when man and woman are in nature's
divine temple.

We are celebrating our love for each other.

Even the Gods are impressed, nature seems to respond
with approval, as we build in our passion for pleasure.

We lie in the darkness and our bodies breezily glide
towards each other.

We are so close, every vital moment filled with such
loving intensity, we are so alive, invigorated and in
absolute deep love.

This love swells like the ocean, it knows no bounds or
constraints.

As our enthralment grows, we begin to soar as if we
might reach those stars bejewelling the sky above us.

We melt into the earth but rise to the heavens.

This moment is full of such sweet rapturous pleasure
and transporting euphoria.

I am mesmerised by you and this divinity we share.

The trance-like elation I feel in each glorious moment
of togetherness and touching of bodies, hearts, minds, our
souls are making love under the cosmos, as if in a
creational myth.

We float in a cloud of unbridled delirium, as we
explode towards the heavens in a deep rumbling quaking
glorious release.

True Love's Desire.

When we make love we take our time, there is no rush.

We start by communicating with our eyes.

Our eyes speak our true love's desire for deep unwavering connection.

This longing and fascination for each other builds into a heavenly desire to reach out and touch each other.

Slowly, we begin to caress each other in a very gentle, floaty delicate and breezy way.

We are swaying with our hands from head to base.

We surrender, completely, to this moment and this complete love.

The electricity begins coursing throughout our core, descending down from heart and rising up from the base.

We are creating a current of magnificent and powerful energy between us.

Our bodies are lit up and on fire and we progress to join each other as our bodies are craving and pulling for each other's fusion.

There is a need and calling to enter each other.

Our bodies want us to engage deeply with each other.

Our focus shifts to the sacred place and space of deepening connection and consciousness.

Our bodies are now awake and in their full power and
want to join and merge.

Slowly and careful inch by inch we unite, as I feel you
rise and uncoil with such incredible energy.

The warmth and luscious power you possess is
enticing and healing at every movement you make.

We radiate a warm and golden glow as our bodies
ascend into an ethereal glow.

Waves of Cascading and fluttering pleasure from the
divinity and beauty of this moment.

We are enraptured by our magnificent love for
each other.

We are completely contained and encircled by
spiralling energy and heat.

This love which is so pure, simple, untainted and real.
A love of the soul.

Sacred Moment.

When we make love our entire bodies join, as one glorious temple of electrical passion.

We savour every part of each other, as we focus on loving every part of each other's body completely, utterly and with great remembrance.

We fuse gently together and breathe in unison.

The only expectation is of completely unwavering adoring love and worshiping each other in our divinity.

We take our time, we have hours to touch, caress, massage and devour each other's skin.

We relish in every sensory pleasure, which is ignited by our deep love for each other.

There is no end game, just the heavenly blissful eternal now.

We are focussed on just each other in deep devotion like prayer.

Love is prayer and prayer is love.

We surrender ourselves to each other as we gently feel the rise and fall of every breath and the divinity of this sacred moment together.

Tantilise.

Tantalise me slowly with your kiss.

Kiss me from my neck, all the way down my body.

I will allow you to steward the experience entirely.

I close my eyes and feel my skin reacting to you kiss
and gently caress my temple.

You undress me so sensually and with great care, you
savour every moment we have together.

The thrill of being so worshipped by your lover, warms
your core essence.

I feel electrified in your arms, as you indulge all my
senses and nerve endings in a slow erotic dance of love.

As our clothes fall away, we slowly take our time. You
are utterly devoted to my pleasure.

As you pamper every inch of my body I am yearning
for you to fill me with your soul.

Intimacy.

The tenderness and intimacy of a kiss.

A gentle invitation to caress another's lips
with your own.

An exquisite exchange of love and bliss.

When lips touch hearts soar and nerve endings tingle in
the sweetness of the moment.

Divine gentleness of a precious encounter between
two souls in love.

A sacred moment to be savoured and felt
and remembered.

My Challis.

The sweetest tingles of ecstasis rise through my body
as you enter me with a divine jolt.

As we gently rock in a smooth rhythmic unison, I can
feel all my nerve endings come alive, in a splendid charge
of energy that is wanting to build through my body.

We stay slow, there is no rush and want to feel and
savour every divine inch of you, as you fill my challis.

My body doesn't want you to leave, it wants to hold
you there tightly.

It wants you to fill me completely and deeply
with your love.

The building is slow, but deep and intense with
delicious sensory pleasure.

The intensity of our love enhances the divinity of
your passion.

We want to consume each other completely.

The crescendo of sensuality is at feverish levels.

Our thirst and erotism is spiralling further beyond
comprehension.

The longing to consummate our love fuels a
thunderous trembling, annihilating release.

We let the waves wash over us and through us until
they final subside in blissful, peaceful loving calm.

Ablaze.

You set me ablaze with your intense burning desire.

The searing heat of our bodies raises to epic proportions.

Your ravenous hunger leaves me craving you wildly.

The deeper you go, the higher I soar in extreme, volcanic ecstasy.

You fill me with your divine love and ignite my entire existence in a fiery explosion of passion

Melt.

Melt into me.

Merge completely.

Let there be no separation.

Let there only be us in this infinite, eternal moment.

Possess all that I am.

Take me completely and absorb me into your loving existence.

Let the nectar of our love consume you entirely.

Let this divine act replenish your thirsty soul, to its heavenly pleasure of existence.

Suchness.

I feel your love enrapturing me, as you cloak me in
your tingling loving energy.

My body rises to the occasion, every part of me is
ready to receive you.

My skin is elevated and electrified by your
soul's presence.

I feel you entering my temple with a holy jolt of
extreme energy and searing heat.

I soar instantly to a great height and float in this
ethereal place, quickly climbing higher and higher exalted
in your loving depths.

My entire chakra system is energised and radiating
immeasurably strong feelings and sensations.

The quivering energy which is building and scaling
rapidly to stratospheric proportions.

Our bodies take flight, in an earth shattering crescendo
of self annihilating bliss and splendid pleasure.

As we collapse spent and blissfully into each other and
merge into suchness.

Surrender.

Surrender to me.

To this moment.

Allow my passion for you to bring you to heavenly
states of release and ecstasy.

Let me consume you with sultry delight.

Surrender to this love.

This love, which is an unstoppable creative force.

This love that soars, expresses and envisions
magnificent beauty.

Submit to me.

Be swept away, in my raging passion for your
very essence.

Let me love every part of you.

Don't hold back.

Release yourself to all that this is and enter the divinity
of our love.

Give yourself to me.

Completely.

Merge with the majestic soul fire of true love.

Love's Essence.

Caress my skin, close your eyes and feel my body raise
in response to your heavenly touch.

Feel every part of me with your eyes closed, map your
hands across the undulating curves of my womanly shape.

Shower me with gentle kisses of your love, as your
warmth fans my flames.

I feel my essence dancing with yours swirling, rising
and uncoiling in this beautiful rendezvous.

Breathe in our love, fill your senses with this airy
romance, abundant with strength and gentleness.

Taste this nectar of sweetness and honey, savour the
divinity of this moment.

Join with me in the grace of this love, immerse in the
holy chalice of life.

Replenish my temple, full and overflowing with love's
divine expression of intimacy and harmony.

Devour Me.

Fill me entirely with your love.

Leave no space unoccupied by your insatiable hunger.

Ravish me utterly and desperately.

Be absolutely consumed by this passion.

I am yours to take.

In the cradle of our existence this love becomes
bountiful and flourishing with extreme sensations
of adoration.

Devour me with every inch of your manhood, make
my body sing until it is breathless and quenched.

Our love is a fusion of divine peaceful beauty and
extreme fiery passionate desire.

Our silken bodies glide rhapsodically in this heavenly
dance of our souls.

They combust in an alchemical build up of pent up
energetic release which is unrestrained and
uncontrollable.

We are explosively powerful deep in our resonance,
causing an entire body spasmodic exhalation.

Safe in others temples we are renewed and healed by
this majestic unconquerable love.

This love is bigger than imaginable and more gorgeous
than any earthly bound human description.

Our love is unconditional and unstoppable.

This love is infinite.

Altar of Devotion.

Tame me with your wild manly essence.

Take control of me and plunge me into the abyss of
ecstasy, unfathomable, engorging and
completely consuming.

Fill me entirely with the intensity of your love.

My entire being surrenders to you in this burning
moment of extreme passion.

You ignite my soul and I am transported to
another dimension.

I lose all sense as you sweep me into an ocean
of exaltation.

You worship my body in its entirety, at this altar of
devotion and divine love.

Your Arms.

In your arms I am released.

I am absolved from all suffering I have ever felt.

I am free to soar like a bird in your arms.

Filled with such immeasurable extasis.

My entire body surrenders in a languid silken release.

I drift in you arms in states of bliss, pleasure and
intoxication of unfathomable heights.

We return to this source of our love in brilliant
blinding abandon.

This love consumes you, to the very depth our essence.

We are engulfed in sensuality and in endless somatic
waves of hedonistic luxury.

This decadent moment gives rise to our majesty and
divinity in ethereal absolution.

Shore's of Love.

Glide into the shores of our love.

As we smoothly flow into a kind of intimacy one will never recover from.

We drift in a vast heavenly ocean of our love.

The utter serenity and pure blissful pleasure of divinity.

I feel held and honoured in the sacred temple of your loving embrace.

True loves dance is searingly wondrous, filled with ecstatic memories and moments which are memorialised for all of eternity.

I love you with all that I am and all I desire to be, infinitely.

Crave.

I want you to taste our love.

Completely.

I want you to savour it and savour me.

Let this love consume you entirely, with such raging
passion, immense intense pleasure.

True love never hides, it is confident and knowing and
consciously aware.

This love is not one for the closet of darkness
and despair.

This love is for the brilliance and blinding light of day.

This love makes you soar to the bright lights of stars,
the sun and the moon.

This love warms you and soothes your soul.

This love is earthy and erotic and powerful
and trembling.

This love will leave you spent, but still craving more.

This love will get into your eyes and under your skin.

There is no place that this love can hide, it's full of
splendid glory and honest pride.

The sensuous heat of this endless romance, has me
adoring your soul in this stirring sumptuous dance.

Coalescence.

We coalesce in the sacred space inhabited only by God.

We are suffused by light and loving energy and
glorious warmth.

This is a journey of loving sensations and
meditational presence.

We are lovingly enveloped in a heavenly space of
our creation.

We are so utterly consumed by each other in this moment.

You gaze with such deep yearning and intensity
into my soul.

I feel my kundalini tingle as it rises and spreads throughout
my chakra system and into yours.

The sultry feeling of our skin touching, frictionless,
smooth and soft like a silken flower petal, so gentle
and devoted.

Your aroma fills my senses with your presence; your
delicious essence takes me to greater heights.

The gentle sound of your breath fills me with such
adoration, as all the senses are consumed by this
loving exchange.

We savour and merge in each unifying moment, as we
dissolve and mingle together in this bliss.

In this place you are seen, felt, inhaled, savoured and heard
completely.

This love is a fluid ethereal mélange of delight and
love's purity.

Transcendence.

Transcendence.

When we join in this erotic dance, we transcend this plain of existence.

Our light bodies swirl and merge into a technicolor symphony of our love.

Our love is palpable in this sensual whirlwind of searing emotions and burning love.

Our love has created something more, a moving tapestry of spirituality and artistry.

We fuse into a brilliant light spectrum of sonic waves and alchemical splendour.

We surrender completely and we are found in enraptured and poetic blissful adoration.

We are one. We are love.

Protection.

Protect me in your loving arms, shield me with this
divine adoration we share.

You cradle me in your arms with such loving
tenderness and care.

All the pain and anguish and despair I have ever felt
melts, into the security of our unwavering love
for each other.

We have created a wombic environment for our love to
grow and develop to new heights of existence.

This love is like the rebirth of our souls.

We are in this divine sacred space of nurturing
adoration and comfort.

I release all doubt and give myself wholly to you in
this moment and for always.

This love is greater than us both. This love is
infinite and pure.

This love is heavenly bliss and raging passion.

This love can conquer any fear and this love
will never end.

This love is alchemical bliss which merges into a
cocoon like sanctuary of warmth and glowing radiance of
delight and love's heavenly purity.

Merge.

Merge with me into something more, become something stronger and more beautiful than before.

As we look adoringly deep into each other's eyes, I feel found by you as you envelope and surround me with warmth and intimacy of this moment .

You see me, you feel me, you are me.

There is a calmness as we move in tantric expression and rhythmic motions, the depth of our feelings are sweeping over me in crashing waves of love.

We are so close, I feel your soul and your heart beating in unison with mine and I feel safe here.

I am filled with utter bliss and divine love for you in this moment which spans eternity.

We have expressed our love, in this fully splendid glorious union. I love you beyond words and actions.

Enraptured

Enraptured by you.

As you explore every crevice of my being.

I'm swept away into a dreamy and ethereal cloudscape,
I am no longer in this body.

You savour me like a nectar of a divine fruit you wish
to consume in is entirety.

I am entranced by your masterful deep soulful kiss.

My feminine ambrosia is a delicacy and heavenly
fragrance to be savoured and absorbed.

You treat my body like a luxurious banquet of
heavenly delights.

You indulge and relish in wonderment of our love
and adoration.

You make me journey to the most beautiful realms of
existence and pleasure.

You take me on a soaring flight to quivering ecstasy
and powerful release.

Entranced.

You love me with such depth and exquisite
beautiful passion.

You cradle me in your arms wanting to be as close as
our bodies will allow.

Your skin is like silk to touch and sends beautiful
waves of euphoria throughout my body at every caress.

We cling to each other as if entranced in
our lovemaking.

You fill me with sumptuous joy and abundant pleasure,
in this land of milk and honey we are indulging in.

We are immersed in this beautiful love of each other.

We are utterly consumed by each other's hearts, minds
and bodies.

As our souls opulence and plentitude of their
satisfaction cries in rapturous wonder.

This is a glorious expression of our adoration for
each other.

We are making such splendid and musical
remembrance, to be treasured and savoured for eternity.

Vessels.

Our bodies are exquisite vessels of our divine love
for each other.

We are enraptured and utterly consumed, by higher
euphoric states of consciousness.

When we join, our souls fuse and become an expansive
love, beyond the confines of this human existence.

The excitement and sensitivity of you finding the
depths of my existence, makes me soar in the sky like an
erupting star.

The pleasure and devotion you bestow on me makes
me long for you never to leave this vessel.

This sacred space we share is full of elemental fire and
holy truths of a deeper knowing.

This love is giving birth to something entirely new, this
love is an incubus of immortality.

The tension of heat drives us to angelic heights, only
Gods dare tread or even know.

The way we make love is an artistic canvas of sounds,
textures, colour and musical vibrations.

As we bend and contort in a fluid mass of ecstasis and
explosive powerful release.

Intoxication.

You fill me with sweet tingling ecstasy, as we merge into delicious depths.

We are closer together than known, as one trembling soul unified in glorious oneness.

There is a profound sense of infinite love we feel for each other in this moment.

We have become a swirling and pulsating flow of beauty and harmony.

As our bodies collide in an epic dance of passion and soul stirring rapture and euphoria.

Our temples are burning with elation, as if in a trance of our love and blissful happiness.

We are so content in this sacred space, which allows such beauty and self expression.

We are enticingly swept and surrounded by each other, in the altar of loving artistry.

We are absolutely intoxicating deep in our essence.

We see stars in each other's eyes and are transported to higher states of being and feelings, which explode into the madness of a quaking, earth shatter release.

Cascading Love.

The moment you enter me, I become charged and alive
and filled with spiralling strength and hunger for you.

I am being filled by your love in its entirety.

Waves of passion and adoration cascade throughout
my existence.

My soul soars to heights of magical delight and waves
of vitality.

I am swept away in the alchemy of your love
and passion.

Our love is a visual Synesthetic field as our sensory
field lights up in pure unbridled connection.

I submit and surrender in entirety to your
loving control.

As I all lose control, absolute pleasure takes over and
courses through my entire being in cosmic waves of
ecstatic pleasure.

As my eyes shut I am transported to another realm of
existence where I explode in the pureness of this love
which has become larger than quantifiable.

We merge into this divine love with unstoppable
power, beauty of veneration and all consuming love.

Deep.

When you stare deep into my soul, the heart of my
existence I know I am home.

I know that you truly love me with every single ounce
of your being.

In this moment, you know unequivocally that there is
no other woman for you.

That magnitude of you entering my soul, with a
powerful jolt.

I feel the whole room fade from view as I am swept
away, instantly into the rhythm of our soul dance.

You move through me so smoothly, artful and with
intensity beyond description.

My body is your altar and you are devoted to
its worship.

Feverishly, I feel our temperatures rising as every
nerve ending is ascending to explosive combustion.

Our bodies are like an earthquake of energy,
thunderously shaking with volatile and climactic release.

In this moment, we are restored and infinite.

Touch Me.

Touch me.

Touch me on every inch of my skin.

Envelope me in your loving caress.

Glide your hands over my smooth skin, and watch it
rise in electrical delight.

Start with your lips.

Kisses of loving delights.

As my warmth rises use your tongue, cover me in the
sensuality of your love.

Love me from base to crown.

Endow me in sweet ecstasy.

Inhale my undulating body in sweet blissful tingles and
smouldering heat.

Consume me whole, utterly and completely.

Electricity.

From the moment our skin meets, an electrical current courses through our entire beings.

The deliciousness of touching each other, the closeness, the togetherness, the oneness, the splendour.

This is a fusion of our soul, well beyond any luminous earthly delight.

You make me soar, rapidly into the stratosphere of our love with explosive hunger.

Every motion and touch is electrifying, lighting up our soul a raging fire to the depths of our hearts.

This glorious love can not be contained.

It wants to run wild and free and to erupt in an exquisite intimacy.

Our souls have no boundaries when we are in this sacred yoke, replenishing ourselves in this divine source of life.

Our earthly bodies melt and merge into a humid refuge of our love.

No one can reach us, we are safe together, as we glow in the sanguine haze of passion.

Primordial Love.

Our love is primordial, it is as old as the
universe's existence.

As you caress my body I feel the wind stir in a tempest
delight as it swirls around our bodies and entire existence.

The heat of our burning purple flame rises through the
root to crown in an alchemical fire of supreme heat.

We are bound by the earthly delights of the sultry
connection to our source of origin.

As the waves of love encase our bodies we glide into
an explosive rhythm or scalar proportions.

This is live and divine existence encapsulated.

This is source and origin as we return in fits of ecstasy
to a play of abundance and calm.

Cocoon.

Our love is primordial, it is as old as the
universe's existence.

As you caress my body I feel the wind stir in a tempest
delight as it swirls around our bodies and entire existence.

The heat of our burning purple flame rises through the
root to crown in an alchemical fire of supreme heat.

We are bound by the earthly delights of the sultry
connection to our source of origin.

As the waves of love encase our bodies we glide into
an explosive rhythm or scalar proportions.

This is live and divine existence encapsulated.

This is source and origin as we return in fits of ecstasy
to a play of abundance and calm.

The Destination.

Sometimes the end destination is much better than
the journey.

Save yourself for a man.

Wait to feel him.

Savour every exquisite moment.

What is the true home feeling when his soul enters you.

Souls become entwined in an alchemical fire.

When you commingle in other realms and states of
being you truly understand the divine and divinity.

When time stands still and does not exist any longer.

Do you enter a true holy space reserved for only a few,
the sacred chalice of a woman's very existence.

What kind of thrills of existence and ecstasy
are possible.

Earth shattering, heart quaking and universe
making, love.

From the moment our skin meets, an electrical current
courses through our entire beings.

The deliciousness of touching each other, the
closeness, the togetherness, the oneness, the splendour.

This is a fusion of our soul, well beyond any luminous
earthly delight.

You make me soar, rapidly into the stratosphere of our love with explosive hunger.

Every motion and touch is electrifying, lighting up our soul a raging fire to the depths of our hearts.

This glorious love can not be contained.

It wants to run wild and free and to erupt in an exquisite intimacy.

Our souls have no boundaries when we are in this sacred yoke, replenishing ourselves in this divine source of life.

Our earthly bodies melt and merge into a humid refuge of our love.

No one can reach us, we are safe together, as we glow in the sanguine haze of passion.

Smooth.

I smoothly glide up to you and join you.

Your warm essence flows through me with
volcanic heat.

We pause and savour this sweet moment of unbridled
sensorial ecstasy.

Every nerve ending of my body is ignited.

Single Moment.

I love it when you caress my body, you work you way
down my body from my lips to my divine origin.

You are tantalising me, you electrifying me with waves
of tenderness and euphoria with every single moment.

Create.

I love those deeply intimate moments when you
penetrate right into my soul with equal force to that
of your gaze.

Mesmerised by the love we share and create together

Touching.

Love making is for any room, not just a bedroom.

The best thing about love is it can inspire
you anywhere.

Those moments where intimate tenderness turns into a
sensual longing.

Touching each other becomes an erotic experience.

A cuddle turns into a deep body embrace of emotions
and motions.

You completely lose the complete context of where
you are other than being with each other completely and
utterly immersed in love.

Trembling Nervousness.

When you first touch me I tremble with nervousness
and excitement, that indescribable feeling of electricity
charges through my veins and chakras.

My entire being aches with burning desire but we
patiently take our time.

So much longing and love we share that it consumes
us completely.

Adam and Eve.

You take off your board shorts and insist I
join you now.

Together like Adam and Eve we walk into the tropic
sweltering woods.

You can't resist my body and you quickly pin me to
a palm tree.

I can't resist your throbbing manhood. You swiftly and
agilely enter me.

The fear of being caught in daylight makes it so
tantalising erotic.

I forget everything as we explode in ecstasy together.

Then walk out naked into the water again, so
innocently like nothing happened.

Dunes.

We walk to the sand dunes you point. This is the spot.

At high noon you have a high time deep in me. You
passionately fill me completely with your love.

So filled with desire, sweat, sun and sex with explode,
as the waves crash in front of us.

Sinful Delight.

I like to perform for you with another woman.

Watching us together drives you wild with desire.

But you can't touch, you can only look at her pleasure.

A woman exploring another woman in ways a man
doesn't know how.

But you want to learn. You are beside yourself and
rock hard with wanton lust.

I make you take her, but she doesn't want you.

She likes women, she wants me to herself.

And you don't want her, you want me all to yourself.

You demand entry and gently push her aside as she
continues to touch me in places you can't reach.

She wants me to pleasure her.

We all fall in a heap of sinful delight.

Fruit.

I love it when you take me from behind, such a primitive and animalistic way to take woman. Raw rugged and a masculine style ape like and guttural.

When you enter it inflames me, immediately my flower begins to bloom out. This is how you make a woman's origins fruit.

As you explore me from behind my womanhood becomes dripping, engorged like a juicy peach full of heavenly sweet nectar, ripe for plucking and entering.

Longing.

That deep longing gaze of intimacy, loves looks.

We hold our gaze of deep love, soul connection and
unbridled affection.

Unafraid, we see the truth of our love.

There is no illusion or delusion.

Real lovers can't be found, they are already deep inside you.

When we join, it is like we never did not exist together.

We carry our loving intensity into the stratosphere, soaring into the
greatest spaces.

This love is not messy, this love is smooth and sultry and
oh so sexual.

This love is connected and deeply ingrained in our core essence.

This is the loving space; it is divine sexuality, of desire
and oneness.

Incandescent Desire.

That divine jolt, as your soul smoothly enters my
holy temple.

The feeling my body experiences as all the nerve
endings deeply tingle through my entire
womanly essence.

A ripple is sent up my earthly being, from my root to
crown chakra as all our cosmological nerve endings align
and connect into a slow and hot rocking alignment.

I'm filled with so much sweet ecstasy, my mouth falls
open in divine pleasure of being filled and incandescent
desire for more loving replenishment

We make musical movements as our rhythm changes,
filled wholly with a trembling orchestral act of giving
and receiving.

A divine love making act of unity and integration.

Until at last, we are both left spent, quivering , naked,
whole and in throbbing, burning ecstasy of heavens
awakening within us.

Naked Dance.

I want to dance naked with you.

I want to wrap my nakedness all around you and
envelop you completely in our love.

I want to tangle messy or awkwardness and limbs and
sweetly scented bodies.

I want you to fill me up so completely and then allow
me to lose all sense of inhibitions.

I want your soul to explode into the cosmos with mine.

I want to melt into your arms, but still want
more..... I want....

Tangled.

Tangled brilliantly soaring up through the visceral
cosmological plane.

Our bodies entwined so deeply, connected by an
unbreakable

Fire bond.

My power is strengthening and kundalini surges and is
ready to explode.

Envelope.

We envelope each other in a cosmic womb of
sensory delights.

All my nerve endings are exploding with electric
charge from your caress.

We are skin on skin, but we want to get closer still.

Engulfed in a heady swirl of passionate
rhythmical dancing.

Our body's gently collide in an all consuming feast of
the heart, mind, body and soul.

Spent.

Spent.

Two bodies.

Two hearts now rejoined.

One soul never separated.

The final frontier of oneness and unity.

The beauty of you, the beauty of me.

The grace and the tenderness, as we fill the room in our
loving poetic ecstasy.

Our love is as deep and as vast as the cosmological
ocean, the very seed of consciousness, life and
creativity itself.

Divination.

There is no place unexplored, our bodies the map of pleasure and erotism.

You turn me around with deep probing and pulsing desire.

An acrobatic tantric manoeuvre of curving limbs and loving explosive exploration.

Every inch navigated with curious intent and unmixed devotion.

So unified, we become one writhing form of quivering energy and divination.

Lustful Hands.

Lustful hands full of passion and strength touch my body in all the right ways and in all the right places.

I meld into the shape I need to become.

I'm like a liquid pool of sexuality and energy overflowing with longing and wanting.

Electricity flows through my core essence into your body with enough passion to light up the stars.

My very essence has a throbbing heartbeat of its own ready to explode.

Liquify.

When we touch we liquify into some other unworldly
substance, of the most delicious consistency.

Our bodies like a malleable liquid, a molten lava
pool of love.

Burning white hot with love, desire and lust.

I'm not sure where you begin, and I end.

It's a formless, edgeless field of energy merging in
divine splendour.

Swirling Ecstacy.

The anticipation of your touching me fills me with so
much warm delight, love and searing desire.

I feel the energy from your fingertips flow
through my core.

Swirling ecstasy vibrates around my existence as you
join with me.

My whole body lights up in pleasure from root to
crown in intoxicating rhapsodic release.

The room fills with vibrant exploding colour and light
as we are transported into another dimension of pure love.

Devour Me.

I want you to devour me.

Every moment and inch of my body to be mapped by
your tongue.

I want you to feel me.

Every crevice and gradient of my skin.

I want you to devour me.

The sweet, the salty and the sultry.

I want you to fill me.

With your love and energy until I overflow in ectstasy.

Love's Altar.

Kneeling at the altar of love

I appreciate all that I am and all that you are.

Two divine vessels of uniquely, beautiful, powerful souls.

Love's dance is of cleansing and catharsis.

Of release, of growth.

Of understanding and supporting.

Of divine unconditionally acceptance and love.

Of beauty and grace.

Of raw and untethered feelings and emotions.

Unconditional support and ascend growth.

Of unbreakable connection and unwavering adoration.

True ltove of the soul, like no other

Cosmological Force.

Our love is a beautiful bright burning flame of love.

Our passionate and inquisitive souls have the desire to light up every shadow with the sheer brilliance of our illuminating light.

The glow of our love can surely be seen from space.

When you take me in your arms our energy exchange instantly ignites into a flame of intense love, connection, passion and unbridled want.

We are an unstoppable, magnetic, cosmological force.

Beloved.

I feel in love with your energy, not the way you look.

From the moment I encountered you I have magnetically been pulled towards you and my path is like a journey through the matrix, the synchronicity I experience verifying the path.

This is quantum entanglement.

On our initial encounter my heart stopped and then reset. It was the electric boost I needed to get me through the soul challenges and karmic physics I've needed to learn, understand and heal. This will enable me to fix this for others.

You are my other half, I love you and I let you go and surrender to this process completely. I commit and honour our soul contract.

Namaste my beloved.

Rainy Days.

I love those blissfully rainy days where we sleep in late and just stay in doors and watch our favourite films in comfy clothes.

We snuggle up on the couch and kiss like teenagers trying to learn self control. But there is nothing controlled about our passion for each other.

I feel you gaze on me not the film and you gently kiss me and slowly put your hand on my tummy. I feel your hand gently and smoothly glide up towards my breasts, sweet tingles fill my body and my skin rises in pleasure. We are making our own movie now the sensual up close and personal kind. You ease my clothes off and stare at my naked body in the morning night with great satisfaction. You disrobe and join me completely naked and filled with adoring love and passion.

These encounters fill me with warmth and safety, cocooned away in our lovers nest savouring every kiss, every touch, every stroke, every moment of pure unadulterated bliss.

Rhapsodic Bliss

Love is surrendering into the moment.

Love is the freedom to be you and express yourself completely and fully without reserve or hesitation.

Moments of ecstasy and bliss spent together devouring each other's very essence. Complete vulnerability and nakedness spiritually, emotionally and physically.

Slow tantric movement where we worship each other and give each other exactly what we crave and desire.

Reckless passion and wild abandon of skin on skin committing every single beautiful sin together. The intense gaze locked on to each other's souls makes it deeper, sweeter, longer and more intense as our souls merge into one unified love once more.

The stars shatter, minds explode and the worlds very existence shakes in quaking annihilating glorious rhapsodic bliss.

Consumed

I love it when you take me by surprise.

Those times when you come up behind me like a man completely possessed.

Those times when your inner beast takes over and takes control.

These are the moments where I completely surrender to the unbridled passion burning in our souls.

Still clothed you reach for me and my unquenchable womanly essence.

This is raw and masculine sensation, you firmly but respectfully take what is yours and what you desire.

I am completely under your spell and filled with passionate wanton lust.

These are the times of desperation where you can't get enough of each other.

You can't be consumed enough.

The times where no bed is involved, but a natural environment.

The thrill of being outdoors and completely consumed by you.

Summer.

I love the smooth, sexy, sultry, summer feeling
with your lover.

Your skin has been sun-kissed with sun, surf and sand.
You feel that sexy summery feeling of sensuality
over flowing.

You glide into the shower and feel the smooth stream
slid over your silky glistening skin, as you slip into
shower together.

There's something so steamy and erotic about
showering with your lover.

Your nerve endings are tuned into the pleasure zone.
Senses have been heighten from such a free, uninhibited
day of semi nakedness and frivolous encounters under the
shimmering sun from sunrise to sunset in sand dunes.

It's that feeling of slipping out of the shower to
reclothe and instead sliding on to the bed for a smoothly
orchestrated encounter.

That feeling where you just look at each other and your
kundalini rides through your spine.

You redress but the passionate kisses take ahold and
you can't make it out the door for the longing and deep
physical and mental attraction.

When you tune and connect deeply with a woman's
mind over time before you become lovers, you tune into
her very essence and soul fire.

The tantalisingly good feeling of waiting for the object
of your desire and heart.

Shared deep loving passion makes magical soulful
encounters, in which you leave your body for another
universe, only to return for another trip.

When you eventually make it out for a meal the
temptation erupts to leave again.

Deep mental and chemical encounters with another are
what life is made of, what you wait for, what you live for.

Those that hold you in the reality of real
love and desire.

Not an ephemeral fleeting passing lustful moment. But
a soul connection built over significant time, like no other.

Tender Moments.

I love those heart searingly tender moments of
mornings spent with you.

I silently listen to the sound of you sleeping, so
peaceful and content.

I look over and see the gentle rise and fall of your
manly chest.

While you sleep I silent wander over to the window
and look out.

You stir slightly and a small moan escapes your lips.

I return to you and gently place my hand under you
chin and give you a gentle kiss on your lips.

I feel you stirring, you kiss me gently back but with
more passion.

Without opening your eyes you slow guide me
back to you.

Our kisses become more intense, each one a passionate
expression of love.

What few clothes we have melt away to skin on skin.

The warmth of your body beneath and gentle caresses
stokes the fire in my soul.

As I feel my heat rising in heady morning passion and
reckless loving abandon.

Abundance.

Just one look at you and my heart swells with
abundance love and desire.

My feelings take flight as I draw you in for a
delightful nuzzle.

Your warm endearing gaze makes me bite my lip in
tantalising anticipation of what comes next.

Beautiful moments of sweet tingling sensations that
feel better than ecstasy.

Smoulder.

That kind of kiss.

The smouldering kind.

The kind that makes butterflies appear deep inside you.

The kind that drives up from your root and release
ecstatically through your crown and then returns in a
spiralling serpentine sensation.

The kind where the entire room disappears from view.

The kind where the sweet tingles of ecstasy leave your
lips and quickly spread throughout your entire body to the
tip of your toes which makes them curl.

The kind that makes your clothes melt away.

The kind that seamlessly ends in a dance.

The kind of kiss that ignites passion and desire throughout your entire soul, you want to explode.

The kind you've waited for your whole life.

The kind that melts the stars and sends you into another dimension.

The irresistible kiss of true lovers bliss, of anticipation and patience and yet uncontrolled fire.

An uncontrolled fire which can't be extinguished which smoulders deeper, hotter, sweeter to the core of your being and very life force of existence.

That's fire.

That's love.

That's passion.

That unquenched thirst.

That's twin flame love.

www.ingramcontent.com/pod-product-compliance
Lightning Source LLC
Chambersburg PA
CBHW071433130726
47997CB00006B/2067